Harold Archermouse

First published in Great Britain in 2014

Text and illustrations © Sally-Ann Warner 2014

For my Mum, Eveline.

Harold Archermouse
and the
White Hare

A Winter Fable

This book belongs to

....

Light snow had fallen on Whispering Wood, making it sparkle in the early winter sun.

All the animals were preparing for frosty weather by collecting food for their cupboards and bringing moss into their homes to keep them warm. The days were now short and cold and the nights were long and dark.

Harold Archermouse poked a whiskery nose out of his front door under Fourstep Bridge.

'Brrr,' he thought, 'the air is chill,

snow has fallen on Tall Tree Hill.

To see my friends I'd planned to go,

if I can make it through the snow.'

Harold picked up his bow and arrows, strapped them to his back and pulled on his fluffy winter boots.   He was off to visit his friends, the hares, who lived on Tall Tree Hill. The hill swept up from the wood towards the sky and everyone could see the single tree, standing like a giant, at the top. It was under this tree where White Hare lived.

White Hare was very, very old and for as long as anyone could remember, he had watched every Round Moon float across the night sky. White Hare watched his moon to be sure that it was always safe and didn't fall from the sky.

The animals of Whispering Wood knew that there were many moons, all of them different; some were thin and curved, some looked like half a coin and others were egg shaped.

All were made of silver and very special.

The hares were the Moonkeepers and each moon had its own keeper to guide and protect it. Every night one of the hares would sit on top of the hill to watch closely as his moon crossed the starry sky.

Harold loved to visit and sometimes sat with the hares to help them keep watch.

He scampered around the bottom of Tall Tree Hill and through the snow towards the hares.

'What's this?' he thought as he looked down,

'It looks to me like a silver crown.'

Harold picked up a circle of silver from the snowy ground. Around its middle were pictures of moons and stars. It wasn't a crown, but a silver necklet worn by a Moonkeeper; surely they wouldn't lose something so special?

'I'll take this with me and ask the hares if this necklet is one of theirs.'

He hooked the silver circle over his shoulder and ran up the hill. In the distance he saw them. Long ears twitched and many golden eyes turned towards Harold as he went to join the hares.

'It's only Harold,' they said in despair,

'We thought you may be the great White Hare.

For three long days he's been away,

it's not like him to go astray.'

Harold held out the silver necklet and they sadly gazed at it. They told him that it belonged to the most important of them all, White Hare. One of the Moonkeepers said,

'I saw White Hare three days ago,

He was old and tired and moved so slow.

He said it was his time to leave

and left the hill I do believe.'

White Hare was the keeper of the Round Moon, the most amazing and magical of them all.

It filled the sky with silvery light as it rose into the darkest of nights. Its magic pulled the seas up on the beaches and pushed them back again. It helped the baby plants grow up from the soil and it shone on the fields so the farmers could gather crops late into the night.

Everyone loved Round Moon and everyone loved White Hare.

'Perhaps he's resting,' Harold said with a sigh,

'until his moon is in the sky.

Just wait a while, we'll all take turns

to sit on the hill until he returns.'

Harold was a very helpful mouse and was the first to sit under Tall Tree to look out for White Hare. All day he sat on the cold, snowy hill, but there was no sign of him. That night was the night of the Oval Moon and its Moonkeeper was sitting and waiting for it to rise into the sky. Harold decided to go back home and return the next day.

Snuggled down in his warm, cosy bed, Harold fell fast asleep and dreamed.

In his dream the sea had stopped moving, the plants did not grow and the night was very dark, so dark that he could not see if a fox was creeping up on him.

He suddenly woke and thought,

'Oh my goodness, I really must try

to hang a moon up in the sky!

No Round Moon would be so bad

and make the animals very sad.'

Harold set off at once to find something round and bright to hang in the night sky.

By now, many of the animals had heard about White Hare. They started to gather at Tall Tree Hill to look out for him. Everyone was worried that the night would be very dark if he didn't return.

Harold was walking beside the Stream of Dreams, looking and thinking, looking and thinking. He could not find anything round and bright to hang in the sky. Suddenly, a voice called to him from the water,

'Harold, Harold, come here to me!

I've something here you may like to see.'

Harold looked down into the stream and saw his friend, Salmon. In Salmon's mouth was the biggest, most beautiful pearl he had ever seen.

'Salmon, my friend, what a beautiful thing,

a wonderful pearl, fit for a king.

May I take it to place in Tall Tree,

a new Round Moon for all to see?'

Harold thanked Salmon for his lovely gift and carefully rolled the pearl all the way up the hill to where his friends were waiting. Seeker the Hawk saw Harold pushing the large pearl and flew over to help him. Harold said,

'On the highest branch of that tall tree,

please place the pearl for all to see.

Tomorrow night will be just fine,

our new Round Moon will shine and shine!'

Seeker picked up the pearl and flew to the top of Tall Tree. He placed the pearl so it could be seen by everyone watching far below. But Harold and his friends were very sad, the new moon looked tiny when it was so far away, it was just a shiny little dot in the tree.

Now, Harold Archermouse was a very brave and helpful mouse who always did his very best, he was not going to give up easily and decided to look again after lunch. He scampered home and took a large slice of cheese out of his cupboard. Harold sat down to eat his lunch when another idea popped into his head.

'Cheese! Of course - big and round!

And I know where it can be found,

A big white cheese I will go and borrow

to hang up in the tree tomorrow.'

The next day, while the farmer and his wife were feeding their sheep, Harold and his friends carried a round cheese out of the farmer's house. The white cheese was HUGE and needed many little mice to push and roll it up the hill. It was far too big for Seeker to carry into the tree, so Harold took out his bow and arrow. He tied a spider-web rope to the arrow, pulled back the string of his bow, aimed and fired. The arrow carried the rope up into the air, over Tall Tree, and back down to the ground.

'Now the cheese we must lift high,

just like a moon up in the sky.

To help it reach the highest height

we have to pull with all our might!'

Harold tied the rope around the cheese and everyone started to pull on the other end. Very slowly, the big cheese rose into the tree. When it reached the top, Harold tied the end of the rope to a rock and stood back to look at their new moon. Everyone thought it was very good - big, round and bright. They were pleased to have a moon ready for the following night.

It was late afternoon now and very cold, so everyone decided to go home, happy that Harold had come to the rescue. Suddenly there was a shout,

'The crows, the crows, they are eating the moon!

There will be nothing left quite soon!'

Harold and his friends were very sad, the greedy crows had eaten the big white cheese and their moon was gone. Tired and unhappy, everyone went home.

Harold ate his supper and went to bed where he fell fast asleep and dreamed. He dreamed of moons and hares, shiny pearls and giant cheeses, greedy crows and Arthur Smithmouse.

Arthur Smithmouse? Harold woke next morning and thought,

'Arthur Smithmouse in my dream?

I wonder what that thought could mean?

Arthur works with copper and tin,

shiny metals, beaten thin.

Shiny metal! That's the clue!

Now I know what I must do.'

Harold had a brilliant idea. He jumped out of bed and scampered off to the home of Arthur Smithmouse.

Arthur was busy in his workshop. A roaring fire burned in one corner and he was making a metal bowl using a hammer and some shiny tin.

A breathless Harold arrived and Arthur said,

'Hello there Harold, I'm sorry to hear

that old White Hare has disappeared.

It's quite a worry that late tonight

There'll be no Round Moon to give us light.'

Harold told Arthur of his idea. He asked him to make a big, shiny circle of tin to hang in Tall Tree. It would be just like the moon and everyone would be happy again. And that is exactly what Arthur did.

He made the biggest, roundest moon anyone had ever seen.

Later that day, Arthur, Harold and all their friends lifted the giant tin circle above their heads and carried it to the top of Tall Tree Hill.

Harold used his bow and arrow and spider-web rope to pull it into the sky. The low, winter sun shone on the silvery moon. It looked big, round and very shiny. It was perfect and everyone was happy. Now the seas would move again, the baby plants would grow and the farmers would be able to work in the fields at night.

'Well done Harold! Such a good idea!

Tonight the animals have nothing to fear.'

It was getting late and the sun was about to set. Everyone decided to stay

for a while to see their new Round Moon in the night sky. They all

watched and waited, watched and waited. But, when the sun disappeared,

so did the light on the tin moon; it didn't shine anymore and no one could

see it in the night sky.

'Oh dear! Our moon has lost its glow,

where it's gone, we do not know.

It's very dark, we should not roam,

let's go back to our safe, warm homes.'

Poor Harold, he had tried so hard to help. White Hare had not returned,

night had come, and there was no Round Moon.

Everyone walked sadly home across the cold, crisp snow.

Harold was very tired as he walked home, so he sat down to rest on a stone next to Puddle Pool. He thought about the three moons he had tried to put in the sky and a tear trickled down his long furry nose and off the end of a whisker into the pool, making a circle of little ripples.

'I will find a way to help my friends,

I won't give up till the very end.

Tomorrow morning I'll try and try

To hang a moon up in the sky.'

Harold looked at the dark clouds reflected in the pool.

Slowly, the clouds moved away and there, shining in the clear water was the Round Moon.

Harold looked up and there it was. Round Moon was shining brightly across the fields and the woods.

'It's back, it's back! Round Moon is here!

Now all is well, no need to fear!

But is it real, or is it a dream,

for old White Hare cannot be seen?'

He looked down again into Puddle Pool and there, reflected in the water, was White Hare - he was leaping across the great, silvery Moon!

White Hare was not lost; he had gone to live with his moon so that he could look after it forever.

 'He is not lost, White Hare is found,

leaping across the moon so round!

And now it's safe, thanks to Hare

who will always keep it in his care.'

Harold was so happy that he laughed and giggled and jumped up and down. In fact, Harold was *over the moon*!

'Good things happen when you don't give up.'

Printed in Great Britain
by Amazon